Bagheera was searching for Mowgli.
He heard a loud trumpeting noise.
It was the Elephants.
They were marching through the jungle.
"Perhaps they will help!" cried Bagheera.
He hurried towards them.
He jumped on to a branch.
It hung down over the path.

MOWGLI
FIGHTS
SHERE KHAN

Based on the *Mowgli Stories* by Rudyard Kipling
Told by Jocelyn Phillips
Illustrated by Colin Frooms

PURNELL
London W.1

Mowgli was lost in the jungle.
He had run away from his friends,
Baloo, the Bear, and Bagheera, the Panther.
They were taking him to the village,
but Mowgli didn't want to go.
Foolish Mowgli was in danger.
Shere Khan, the Tiger, was in the jungle.
He hated all men.

The Elephants were singing a marching song.
"Hup, two, three, four,
Keep it up, two, three, four.
Oh, we march from here to there,
And it doesn't matter where.
You can hear us push
Through the deepest bush
With a military air."

"Stop, please!" shouted Bagheera.
At once the Elephants stopped.
"What do you want?" said Hathi,
the leader.
"The man-cub is lost," said Bagheera.
"Will you help me to find him?"
"Right!" roared Hathi. "Forward march!"
The Elephants crashed through the jungle.
The search had begun.

But Shere Khan was listening.
He was hiding behind a tree.
The Tiger licked his whiskers.
He smiled slyly.
"Aha!" he purred. "A man-cub!"
"That will be a tasty treat!"
Softly he padded away.
He would look for Mowgli, too.

Mowgli was tired.
He sat down by a big tree.
Kaa, the Python, saw him.
"S-so nic-ce to s-see you,"
he hissed.
Mowgli turned away.
He didn't like this strange snake.
"Leave me alone," he said.
Kaa swung around in front of Mowgli.

"Trust me," said the Python.
"I'll help you to stay in the jungle."
He turned his strange eyes on Mowgli.
Kaa stared at him.
Slowly he began to sing:
"Trust in me, just in me,
Shut your eyes and trust in me."
Soon Mowgli was fast asleep!

The Python coiled around Mowgli.
He held him very tight.
He carried him up into the tree.
Just then Shere Khan came by.
He saw Mowgli's footmarks under the tree.
He looked up and saw Kaa's tail.
"I'm looking for Mowgli," said the Tiger.
"Do you know where he is?"

"Search me!" said Kaa.

"That's a good idea," said Shere Khan.

"Come closer."

Kaa was afraid of the Tiger.

He swung himself down.

At once Mowgli woke up.

He crawled out on a branch,

far away from Kaa and Shere Khan.

Shere Khan could not see Mowgli.

He was very angry.

He was sure Kaa had caught him.

He flicked his paw at Kaa's nose.

"If you do see him," he purred.

"Make sure you tell me."

"Yes-s-s, of course," hissed Kaa.

The Tiger padded off into the jungle.

Mowgli watched the Tiger go.
He tip-toed up to Kaa.
He gave a great big push.
Kaa fell down into a thorny bush!
"You told me a lie," said Mowgli.
"You said you would help me.
You are a very naughty snake."
Sadly Mowgli set off once more.

He felt very lonely.
He came to a black pool.
He saw some big black birds.
They were sitting on a dead tree.
"Why do you look so sad?" they asked.
"I haven't a friend in the world,"
said Mowgli unhappily.
"We'll be your friends!" said the Vultures.
They all flew around Mowgli.

They flapped their wings.
They made loud croaking noises.
Shere Khan heard them.
"Vultures!" he said slyly.
"I think I'll have a look."
He padded towards the pool.
He saw Mowgli with the Vultures.
He gave a great big "Grr-rr!"

At once the Vultures flew away.

"Aren't you going to run?" said the Tiger.

"I won't run from anyone," said Mowgli.

"You're a brave boy," said Shere Khan.

"I'll give you a chance."

He covered his eyes with his paw.

"I'll count to ten," he said.

"One, two, three . . ." Mowgli didn't move. "*Ten!*"

Shere Khan sprang at Mowgli.

But Baloo was there!
He jumped on to Shere Khan.
"Run, Mowgli!" he cried.
Shere Khan was very angry.
He turned on Baloo with a snarl!
Mowgli ran to the tree.
He tore off a dead branch.
He hit Shere Khan on the nose!

Shere Khan sprang at Mowgli.
Baloo caught hold of the Tiger's tail.
Shere Khan spun about angrily.
He tried to throw Baloo off.
Suddenly Bagheera appeared.
He carried Mowgli away.
"Let me go!" cried Mowgli.
"We have to help Baloo!"

There was a great crash of thunder!
Then a great flash of lightning!
The dead tree burst into flames!
"Get the fire!" cried the Vultures.
"The Tiger is afraid of it!"
Mowgli raced to the tree.
He snatched up a flaming branch.
He ran towards Shere Khan.
He dashed the flames at his face!

"No! No!" roared the Tiger.

Then he ran into the forest.

"We've won, Baloo!" cried Mowgli.

But Baloo was lying on the ground.

Mowgli thought he was hurt.

But Baloo sat up and laughed.

Mowgli gave him a great big hug.

"I won't run away again!" he said.

Baloo, Bagheera and Mowgli went on their way.

Soon they reached the village safely.